PEZZO
THE PEDDLER
AND THE CIRCUS ELEPHANT

Story and Pictures by
Esphyr Slobodkina
Abelard-Schuman
London   New York   Toronto

Early in the morning,
Pezzo the Peddler woke up.
He stretched himself and said,
"The sun will be up very soon,
and I had better be up too!"
He jumped out of bed and began
to dress.

First he put on his socks.
Next he put on his starched
white shirt.
Then he put on his fine black-
and-white pinchecked trousers.
And last he put on his yellow
high-button shoes.
After Pezzo washed, he had his
breakfast, and put on his jacket
and cap.

Then he picked up his wares and
was ready to go to work.

It was a beautiful morning. The sky was clear,
the sun was bright, the air was fine, and Pezzo
was feeling fine, too.

He walked fast—as fast as he could without
upsetting his caps. For, you see, Pezzo was
a peddler who sold caps. Only instead of
carrying the caps in a bundle on his back,
he carried them right on top of his head.

First he had on his own
black-and-white pinchecked cap,
then a bunch of tan caps,
then a bunch of brown caps,
then a bunch of blue caps,
and, on the very top,
a bunch of red caps.

Pezzo was in a hurry. He wanted to get
to town early and sell a lot of caps.
As soon as he reached the first row
of houses, Pezzo began to call out, "Caps!
Caps for sale! Fifty cents a cap!"

But the street was strangely quiet—all the
doors were closed, and all the windows were
tightly shut. No man stopped Pezzo to try
on a cap. No woman leaned out of a window
to see if they were really good caps.

No children ran after Pezzo,
teasing and trying to mimic his funny walk.
There weren't even any dogs to follow him.
Block after block, the streets were quiet
and empty.

But as he came nearer to the Town Square, Pezzo
began to hear sounds of voices and gay music.
"Ah, how foolish of me to forget!" he thought.
"Of course, it must be the County Fair. Good!
Today should be a fine day to sell my caps."

Sure enough, the nearer
he got to the Town Square,
the clearer he saw that it
was indeed a County Fair.

The Ferris wheels turned.
The merry-go-round went
round and round.
The stalls were bright with
flags and streamers.
Everywhere gay, laughing
people were milling around,
dressed in their
Sunday best.

And at the far end of
the Square, Pezzo saw
an enormous
Circus tent.

"Caps for sale!
Caps for sale!"
Pezzo began to call.
But before he
got to saying,
"Fifty cents a cap!"

B-O-O-M!
went a big drum
as the Circus
parade came
around the corner.
And again,

BOOM-BOOM-BOOM!!!

"Oh, well," sighed Pezzo,
"he is bigger than I.
I'll wait until
he is through."

When the big drum went
past, Pezzo began to call,
"Caps for sale!
Caps for sale!"

But once more, before
he got to saying, "Fifty
cents a cap!"
a great big
bass horn came into view,
and began to thump.

OOM-PA-PA! OOM-PA-PA!
OOM-PAPA-PA!
and OOM-PAPA-PA!
and OOM-PAPA-PA!
PA-PA! PA-PA-PAPA-a-a-a!

"Oh, well," sighed Pezzo
again, "he is louder than I.
I can wait until he
is through."

As soon as the big bass horn
went past, Pezzo began to call,
"Caps! Caps for sale!
Fifty cents a cap!"

Only this time what came
around the corner was not
just a big drum or a loud bass horn
but the whole Circus band.

The trumpets shrilled, the trombones blared
and the little piccolos went tweedle-dee-dee!
The big cymbals went B-O-N-G! and
the tiny triangle went P-I-N-G!

"Oh, well," sighed Pezzo for the third time,
"there are so many of them. I'll just have
to wait until they go by. In the meantime, I
might as well enjoy looking at the parade."

He saw the Circus riders prance by on
their plumed white horses.

He saw the fierce lions and tigers, and
the chattering monkeys in their cages.

He saw a truckload of trained seals
and dancing dogs go by.

And then came the rest of the
Circus animals.
Four striped zebras,
three long-necked giraffes,

two double-humped camels,
and one huge elephant.

People around Pezzo were laughing
and cheering.
They seemed to think that
it was a wonderful parade.
And really it was. Even Pezzo
thought so . . .
until he met up
with Jumbo.

Jumbo was the Circus elephant
in the parade.
He was trained to perform tricks
to amuse the crowd.

Sometimes he would simply take
some peanuts from a child's hand
and put them in his mouth.
Sometimes he would fill his trunk
with water and pretend to give
himself a shower bath.
And sometimes he would steal
a hat from a man in the crowd,
try it on his rider's head,
and return it to the stranger.

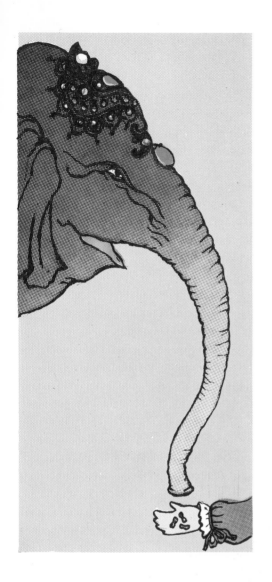

Naturally, when Jumbo saw Pezzo
with his pile of caps, he reached
for it with his long trunk.

In a second, there was a
very surprised elephant,
a very amused crowd, and a
very, very sad peddler.
For all the red caps,
blue caps,
brown caps
and tan caps came
tumbling down in
every direction.

When the tumblers, the jugglers and the clowns
saw all the caps falling, they thought it was a
new trick the Big Boss had added to the parade.
So, each one caught a cap and went on
with his act:

The clowns clowned in brown caps.
The tumblers tumbled in tan caps.
And the jugglers did their juggling
with the red and blue caps.

The crowd roared with laughter. People
shouted and clapped their hands. Everybody
was delighted. That is, everybody except
Pezzo the peddler. He ran after
the parade, calling, "My caps!
My caps! Please give me back my caps!"

But nobody paid any attention to him.
The clowns kept on clowning,
the tumblers kept on tumbling,
and the jugglers kept on juggling....

Down the main street and all around the town,
the parade marched, with Pezzo running after it,
calling, "My caps! My caps!
Please give me back my caps!"

Still nobody paid any attention to him.
Nobody even heard his voice over the loud
noise and din that the animals, the
crowd and the band were making.

At last, Pezzo gave up.
He sat down on a bench
under a big tree and
watched the parade
disappear around the
corner.

When the parade was over, and the animals
were all put away in their stalls and cages,
the Circus People gathered in the
Big Top to congratulate the
Big Boss on his clever new trick.

"Thank you! Thank you, my friends,"
said the Big Boss, "but I don't
know what you are talking about.
Furthermore, whatever it is, I had
nothing to do with it."

"Then who did?"
asked the jugglers.
"Who did?"
asked the tumblers.
"Who did?"
asked the clowns.
"Jumbo did," said Joe,
the elephant rider.

And he told the Circus
People about the little
peddler whose caps Jumbo
had scattered about.

Joe also tried to show
how the peddler
carried all his caps.
But when he got to
the first brown cap,
all the caps fell down.

Then one of the clowns tried to put
on the caps, but when he got to the
first blue cap, all the caps fell down.

Everybody tried.

Even when one of the jugglers tried,
he got to the last red cap,
but again, all the caps fell down.

"Aha!" said the Big Boss. "Perhaps it is
not such an easy trick, after all!"
He sat quietly for a moment and then
continued, "And if it is not such an easy
trick to do, my friends, does it not
belong in the Circus?"

"Yes, yes!" shouted all the Circus People.
So, the Big Boss sent two tall men to find
the little peddler and bring him to
the Circus tent.

As it happened, Pezzo was
not at all hard to find,
for he was still sitting
on the bench under the tree,
thinking his sad thoughts.

"Come quickly!" said the two
tall men. "The Big Boss himself
wants to talk to you."

"Will he give me back my
caps?" asked Pezzo. "All
I want him to do is to
give me back my caps."

But the men just kept repeating,
"Come quickly! The Big Boss
himself wants to talk to you."

So, Pezzo went.

"Hello, there!" said the Big Boss to Pezzo.
"They tell me you can carry all these caps on
your head without ever dropping a single one.
Neat trick, I say, if you can do it!"

"Yes, Sir, I can," said Pezzo.
"In fact, I always do. Like this."

He knelt in front of the caps
and put the bunch of brown
caps on top of the tan caps.
Then he put the bunch of blue
caps on top of the brown caps.
And, on the very top,
he put the bunch
of red caps.

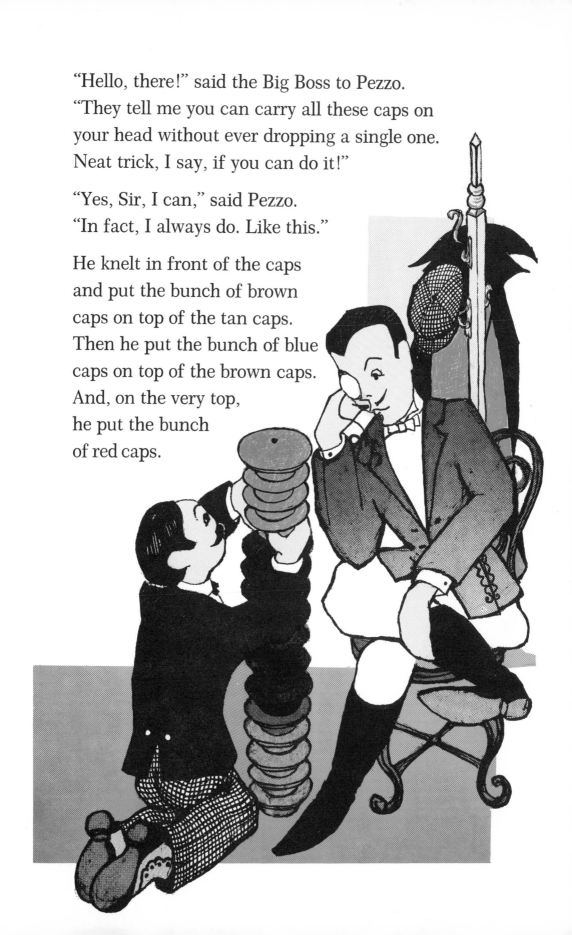

Very carefully, he picked up the whole
pile and put it on top of his own
black-and-white pinchecked cap.

Then slowly, *very* slowly, he got up from his
knees and began to walk around, calling out,
"Caps for sale! Caps for sale!
Fifty cents a cap!"

"Bravo! Bravo!" shouted the Big Boss,
clapping his hands.

"Bravo, bravo, bravo!" shouted the rest
of the Circus People.

"How would you like to do your act in
the Circus Ring?" asked the Big Boss.

"Who? Me?" said Pezzo.

"Of course, you. Nobody else can do it—
believe me, my good man, we tried."

"I...I don't know..." stammered Pezzo.
"I am only a peddler who sells caps.
But if you really want me to...."

That evening, when the Circus lights went on, the show was really grand.

There were horse riders,
and elephant drivers.

There were trained lions and tamed tigers.
There were dancing dogs and talking seals.

There were tightrope walkers,
and jugglers,

and tumblers,

and clowns.

And, of course, there was Pezzo.

Everyone did his act very well.

The crowd clapped and whistled.
But most of all, people liked Pezzo the Peddler.
They clapped and whistled harder than ever,
when they saw how he put on and carried,
on top of his own black-and-white pinchecked cap,
the tan caps,
the brown caps,
the blue caps,
and, on the very top, the red caps,
without dropping a single one.

Pezzo was delighted.
He walked around the
Ring, feeling very straight
and tall, and calling,
"Caps for sale!
Caps for sale!
Fifty cents a cap!"

After the show, Pezzo sold all his tan, brown,
blue, and red caps. Someone even wanted to
buy his own black-and-white pinchecked cap. But
Pezzo wouldn't part with it—it was his lucky
cap, he said. And, besides, it matched
his black-and-white pinchecked trousers.

THE END